A WOODEN SHOE

FOR

NELL

Vicki Johnson & Kelly Walseth

Illustrated by Kelsey B. Anderson

A Wooden Shoe for Nell
From the Poppy's Puppies Series
Published by Poppy's Prints, LLC
poppyandherpups@gmail.com
Saint Paul, MN

Library of Congress Control Number: 2020923544
ISBN: 978-1-7359365-4-3
Juvenile Fiction

All inquiries about this book can be sent to the authors.
poppyandherpups@gmail.com

From the Authors

This book is dedicated to our wonderful paraprofessionals who have been there to support us in our Kindergarten classrooms. Many students have benefited from your loving care.
- Kelly & Vicki

From the Illustrator

For Eli & Jett
- Love, Mom

Poppy the Dog was kind and wise,
With creamy, tan fur and brown sparkly eyes.

A litter of pups had blessed Poppy's heart.
And a story for each would now soon start.

Poppy knew that the world was filled with traditions and fun,
And she wanted each pup to learn about one.

With a lick for a kiss, Poppy nuzzled each pup.
She knew it was time as they looked so grown-up.

She gave a quick bark as she showed them the bag,
That held magical charms to go on each tag.

Their eyes on the bag, each one eager to see,
The pups barked at once, "Which one is for me?"

Poppy picked out a charm and her smile soon grew,
As she showed little Nell a small wooden shoe.

"What's this?" wondered Nell. "My charm is a shoe?"
"Oh, Nell, the Netherlands are waiting for you!"

"To Holland you'll go for Saint Nicholas Day!"
Nell's magical charm then whisked her away.

The shoe charm took Nell to a quaint little town,
Where snowflakes were falling on trees tall and brown.

All the windmills in Holland stood covered with snow,
And bright yellow tulips lay sleeping below.

Nell was then led to a warm, friendly door.
She poked her way in to see a bit more.

A girl spotted Nell first and ran for a hug.
Nell kissed her and circled, then sat on the rug.

The girl said to Nell, "We're preparing for Nick.
There's so much to do for December the fifth!"

The family began with a seasonal song.
The girl cuddled Nell as she barked along.

Then Mama picked up the first box from the pile.
"The bells!" said the children to Nell with a smile.

The little pup saw and felt how the joy spread.
"Ring the bells loudly!" was what Mama said.

Then Nell was surprised! In came a tree.
A tree, inside? But how can this be?

They all taught the pup how to trim it with care,
With bright bulbs and ornaments each branch would wear.

Next it was time for the kids to unwrap,
Their fine wooden shoes from the storage sack.

They polished and shined, and giggled and laughed,
Not one of them noticed the cold winter's draft.

The wood on their shoes began to glisten and glow,
So Nell gave a lick and helped sparkle the toe.

Nell loved the shoes, but what were they for?
She looked at the boy, and he opened the door.

"Go fetch now, Nell!" said the boy to the pup.
She tilted her head and then quickly jumped up.

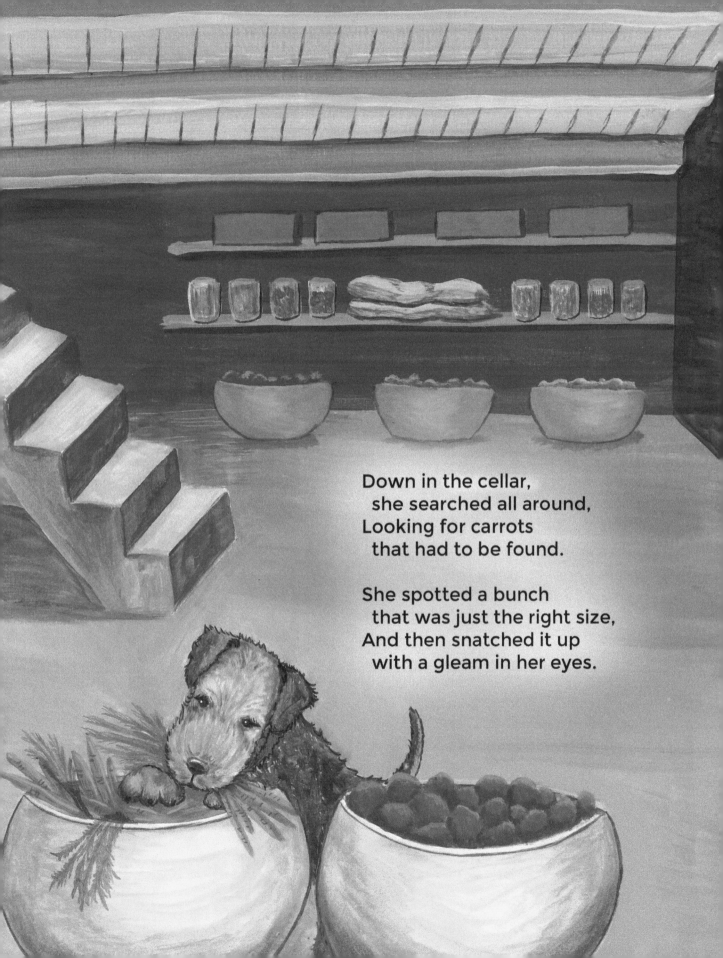

Down in the cellar,
  she searched all around,
Looking for carrots
  that had to be found.

She spotted a bunch
  that was just the right size,
And then snatched it up
  with a gleam in her eyes.

The barn was her next stop for a small bunch of hay.
She raced through the snow and was soon on her way.

She grabbed a mouthful of straw, and was called back quick.
They needed these things to prepare for Saint Nick!

The pup dashed inside and shook snow to the floor.
"Good girl, Nell!" said Mama as she closed the door.

The children were waiting with their clogs by the tree.
Papa poked at the fire and Mama made some tea.

"Hurry, Nell!" shouted the kids with delight,
As the pup brought the treasures she'd found for the night.

The kids took the hay and began stuffing a shoe.
The carrots were next, so Nell joined in too.

Now each clog was ready for Saint Nick's kind horse.
They were placed by the fire, with little Nell's help of course!

The family grew sleepy from their busy day,
So they went off to bed, patting Nell on their way.

And as she tried to keep watch on the shoes,
The warmth of the fire soon put Nell in a snooze.

Then bright rays of sunshine
   were tickling her eyes,
And when she awoke,
   Nell had quite a surprise!

The carrots and hay
   Saint Nick fed to his horse,
Gifting oranges, candies and
   coins of all sorts.

With a bark and a jump, Nell circled with joy.
And soon she was joined by the girl and the boy.

The best part of all was a bone left for Nell,
Because now she had a new story to tell.

She knew that Saint Nick had left her the best treat,
And hoped maybe next year they'd actually meet.

She'd learned about love in this old Dutch tradition.
And now understood her charm's true definition.

The End

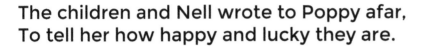

The children and Nell wrote to Poppy afar,
To tell her how happy and lucky they are.

Each family spreads joy in their own special way.
Will you write your tradition and share it someday?

About the Authors & Poppy

Kelly and Vicki are both teachers from Minnesota. They have taught kindergarten together for many years. They have based many of their lessons on good books that get kids excited about learning. Kelly and Vicki also believe that rhyming is one of the foundational pillars of learning to read. They have always wanted to work together on a children's book series. Kelly and her husband have three children. Vicki and her husband have one daughter and are thankful for Poppy. Each puppy in the series is named after someone special in Kelly and Vicki's lives.

Poppy is a Lakeland Terrier. She is full of attitude and thinks she's the boss of the house. She insists on being walked twice a day and is well known in the neighborhood. She has a very gentle side and loves to follow Vicki around wherever she goes. Poppy doesn't have any pups of her own, but if she did, she would want them to learn about traditions around the world.

About the Illustrator

Kelsey is an artist and instructor who specializes in painting, printmaking and photography. As a dual citizen of the U.S. and Australia, she loves traveling and experiencing other cultures and traditions. After reading countless stories with her family, she is excited to illustrate her first children's book. Kelsey lives in Minnesota with her husband, two children, and one spoiled dog.

CPSIA information can be obtained
at www.ICGtesting.com
Printed in the USA
JSHW010750250722
28482JS00001B/1